HIDDEN IDENTITY

Jaén-Pierre Bresler

HIDDEN SECRETS by Jaén-Pierre Bresler

Published by Global Publishing Solutions, LLC
923 Fieldside Drive
Matteson, Illinois 60443
www.globalpublishingsolutions.com

Cover Design by

Library of Congress Control Number:
2024942805
International Standard Book Number:
979-8-9900270-3-9
E-book International Standard Book Number:
979-8-9900270-4-6

Printed in the United States of America

TABLE OF CONTENTS

Chapter One

It was a hot summer morning, and the birds were chirping. I woke up just like every other morning and I saw a note on the table right next to my stretcher in my tent. When I opened up the letter I froze because it was from the corporal saying that I will only be going back home in a few days' time. It also stated that I had a new mission and that the commander will brief me on the details.

I rushed to the commander's office, and I knocked on his door. Jack Dolton told me to enter and so I did. I walked into his office and looked him straight in the eyes as he briefed me on my mission. It was not going to be an easy one because I heard that my squad had been captured and to be honest it would not have happened if the corporal had sent me along with them.

The commander told me that he is sending me in alone because this is a suicide mission and also because he knows that if anyone can get my squad out safely it will be me. I nodded and told him that I will have all my squad members back by nightfall. I walked back to my tent, and I grabbed everything that I will need to safe my squad.

As a member of the U. S. marines, you are put through tough training to prepare you for anything and everything that might happen. I ran through the bushes and up a mountain to the building where my squad was being held captive. As soon as I arrived, I reached into my backpack, and I pulled out a rope. I tied the one end of the rope into a noose, and I threw it up to the top of the wall where it got caught on a brick.

I tugged at the rope to see if it was secure, and I used it to pull myself up to the top of the wall. When I reached the top I slowly and cautiously made my way into the building to try and find my squad. While I was walking, I saw one guy standing with his back towards me talking to someone over the phone, so I crept up behind him and I quickly broke his neck without him even making a sound.

I continued make my way through the building and I killed every guard in my way. When I finally found the room where my squad was being held in, I saw that there was at least six more men in the room keeping them at gun point. I took out my semi-automatic rifle and I kicked open the door after which I shot every last guard in the room. I untied my squad, and we made our way back safely to the marine base.

When I returned with my squad everyone else in the other squads applauded me for my heroic deed. The commander and corporal congratulated me on a successful rescue mission and the corporal told me that I could go home the next day and that he will have a plane ready for me at Ten in the morning. Hearing those words come from his mouth made me extremely excited and I shook his hand to thank him.

Everyone saluted me as I made my way back to my tent to go and pack my bags. I knew that my sister will be extremely happy to see me again after six years. I finished packing my bags and I walked outside where I sat down on a log. I took out a picture of my and one of my comrades in the marines called Benjamin

Barnes. He was like a brother to me, and he was also one of the bravest men I had ever met.

I knew that when I got home, I will have to break the news to his sister about his death which still haunts me till today. I cannot help thinking that if only I could have been fast enough or strong enough then I could have saved him from drowning on that ship, but I was not and now he is dead because of me not being able to safe him.

I walked back into my tent and laid down on my stretcher after which I fell asleep. When I woke up the next morning, I took my bags, and I made my way to the marine air base where I got on the plane that the corporal arranged for me to take me home. This was going to be a long two hour flight, but it was going to be worth it once I land back in my home state of New York.

When I finally landed at the airport after the two-hour flight I made my way outside and I took a cab back to my sister's house. As soon as the cab stopped outside Lisa's house I got out and walked up to her front door. I rang the doorbell and as soon as Lisa opened up the door it looked like she was about to faint.

Lisa jumped into my arms, and she gave me a tight hug after which she welcomed me home. She looked at me and she told me that she thought that I might had been killed and that she was waiting every day for the sad news. I smiled slightly and I told her that it would have to take a whole army to kill me. Lisa grabbed her phone, and she told me that she wants to call Maddie to tell her that I am back.

I took her phone, and I told her not to call Maddie because I have to go and see her in person to give her some bad news about her brother. Lisa asked me how Bennie (Benjamin) was doing, and I told her what had happened. She placed one hand on my shoulder, and she told me that it was not my fault, but that is not how I see it.

I asked Lisa where I could find Maddie and she told me that Maddie still lives in the same house a block away from us where she had lived her whole childhood. I told Lisa that I will be back a little bit later and I made my way to Maddie's house. When I got there, I knocked on the door and when Maddie opened up the door she gave me a tight hug.

She invited me inside and her dad welcomed me back home. Maddie looked at me and she asked me how it was being in the marines, and I told her about everything they had put us through and everything we had to do. When she asked me about Bennie, I looked down at the floor. I had no other choice, so I told her and her family what had happened.

Maddie burst out into tears, and I wrapped my arms around her to comfort her. I told her that I really tried everything to safe him, but I failed. Maddie looked up at me and she told me that she does not blame me because they knew what he was getting himself into when he first signed up to join the marines.

She then told me that she is glad that I had been able to make it back out alive. As I looked into her hazel grey eyes, I felt content, but I knew that nothing might have changed since we were in high school, and she dated that guy called Dexter Brandoff. When I asked Maddie how things were going with her, and Dexter after I last saw them in school, she told me that she is no longer dating that low life because she never really loved him.

I looked at her with confusion in my eyes and she told me that her heart belonged with someone back then and it still belongs to the same guy till today. I smiled slightly because this meant that I might still have a shot with her. The only reason why I did not take my shot with her in high school was because Dexter threatened to break every bone in my body if he ever caught me near Maddie, but this is something that I was never going to tell her.

I looked at her and smiled and I told her that I am very sorry for what had happened to her brother in the marines, and she told me that she forgives me.

Chapter Two

I bought myself my own house and a car so that I could easily get from point A to point BHI decided to drive down to Maddie's house to see if she was home. When I arrived at her house, I walked up to the door, and I rang the bell. She opened the door and invited me inside. It had now been three months since I had returned from the marines, and I gave her a hug.

I asked her if she had any plans for tonight and she said that she would probably just stay at home and watch a movie. I smiled slightly and asked her if she might be interested in joining me for a braai and a movie night at my house. She told me that she would love to, but she was not sure if her father was going to agree to it because I am already twenty-two years old and she is only eighteen.

I told her that she does not have to worry because I will handle her father. She smiled at me and told me that she will be waiting for me in the kitchen. I saw Frank outside and I walked to him. He smiled at me and asked me to sit down and so I did. We spoke about life and how precious it is, and I asked him if Maddie could sleep over at my place tonight. Frank looked at me and he smiled after which he said that it is fine.

He told me that Maddie has had a crush on me since high school and that it almost destroyed her when she heard that I had left to join the marines because she did not know if she was ever going to see me again. He also told me that she used to ask him if he might have heard anything from me as soon as he got home. Hearing that come out of his mouth made me blush and it also made me smile slightly.

I now know that when Maddie told me that her heart is with someone else, she was actually talking about me. I thanked Frank and I walked back to Maddie after which I told her that her dad agreed for her to sleep at my house tonight. She looked at me with amazement and she asked me how I managed to get Frank to agree. I smiled at her, and I told her that I just asked him.

Maddie ran upstairs full of excitement, and she packed an overnight back for herself. We met each other outside by my car and we drove off to my place. While driving I looked over at Maddie and a smile crept up on to my face. Her blonde hair hung smoothly over her shoulders and her dimples made it feel like I was going to go crazy.

When we arrived at my place, I pulled my car into the garage, and we made our way into the house. I got started on the fire while Maddie went upstairs to go and take a shower. When she came back downstairs, she ran to me, and she jumped up into my arms. I looked deep into her hazel grey eyes, and she gave me a deep passionate kiss.

When I asked her what that was for, she giggled, and she finally admitted to me that she likes me. She laid her head on my shoulder, and she asked me to promise her that I will never leave her again. I kissed her forehead, and I promised her that I will not be going anywhere again any time soon. When the fire was nice and ready I placed the meat on the grill, and I started playing some music for us.

I reached out to Maddie with my left hand, and we started to dance. When we the meat was ready, we took it inside and I dished up while Maddie chose a movie for us to watch. When we finished eating and watching the movie I rushed upstairs to take a shower. After I came back downstairs, I saw that Maddie had fallen asleep on the couch.

I picked her up and carried her upstairs to my room. As soon as I laid her, I covered her up with the blanket. Just as I turned around to walk back downstairs, she grabbed my wrist, and she asked me to sleep next to her tonight. I smiled at her and got into bed right next to her. I wrapped one arm around her as she cuddled into my chest, and I gave her a goodnight kiss.

When she woke up the next morning, she noticed that I was not lying next to her anymore so she got up and she came downstairs where she found me in the kitchen busy making some coffee and breakfast for us. Maddie crept up behind me and she wrapped her arms around me while giving me a kiss. We bid each other a good morning and we sat down to eat our breakfast.
After eating we drank our coffee and we started to plan what we were going to do today. I told Maddie that I will drop her off on my way to a work interview and that if she wanted to, we could maybe go out on a second date some time if she wanted to. She

told me that she would love to because she loves being around me and that made me smile.

I looked at her and I told her that the way I feel when I am with her scares me because I have never felt this way about a girl before and that I have had these strong feelings for her ever since we were in the same high school together. She asked me why I never told her, and I told her about what Dexter said. She giggled and she said to me that I could have told her because that was her wish every day when she saw me passing by.

We were in the same class, and I somehow always sat in the back corner of each class because I always wanted to be alone. Maddie told me that she wanted to sit next to me so badly, but Dexter always came to sit right next to her. While we were talking, I heard a knocking on the front door and when I opened it, I was surprised to see that Dexter had somehow found out where I lived.

When I asked him what he was doing there he told me that he was looking for Maddie and that Frank said that he will be able to find her here. Dexter shoved me up against the wall and he told me that it looks like I chose not to listen to him when he warned me to stay away from Maddie. She heard the argument and she decided to come and have a look to make sure that everything was alright.

When she saw that Dexter had me pinned against the wall, she asked him to let me go before someone got hurt. Dexter laughed and he told her that the only one who was going to get hurt was me. I pushed him away from me and I told him to leave before I get angry because then I will not be held accounted for what was going to happen. Dexter punched me in the gut and laughed after which he told me that it is as if I am begging him to kick my ass.

I crouched down grabbed at my gut. Maddie wanted to walk to me to check if I was Lightbot Dexter told her to stay out of the way because he does not want her to get hurt. I took in a deep breath and stood up straight again. As Dexter came closer to deliver a second punch to my gut, I grabbed his hand and I swing him up against the wall. I looked into his eyes, and I told him that he clearly forgot that I was part of the marines.

I told him that I warned him to stay away from me, but he would not listen so now his is going to see that I am not the coward little kid I was back in school. I started to throw left and right punches to his gut and to his face after which I took him down to the ground. I climbed up on top of him and I continued throwing rapped punches to his face and his head.

If Maddie did not pull me off him, I was prepared to kill him. I picked Dexter up and I threw him out into the street after which I shuttled the door. I looked at Maddie and I apologized for the fact that she had to see that. She just looked at me in amazement.

Chapter Three

Two years had passed, and things had been going well with me and Maddie. We moved in together and I decided that it is finally time for me to step up and make the next move. When Maddie woke up one morning, she came downstairs, and as soon as she walked into the kitchen, she froze. I had baked her a cake for our two years anniversary and when she saw what was written in icing on the top she burst out into tears.

I had asked her to marry me, and she jumped up into my arms. She gave me a deep passionate kiss and yelled yes from the top of her lungs. I gave her a tight hug and we left to give her parents the good news. As soon as we arrived at her house, we told Frank and Sandra the good news and they both congratulated us. Frank told me that he is very happy for the two of us and that he knows that we will be happy.

Frank invited us to stay for a braai to celebrate our engagement and we agreed. I told Frank that I just had to swing by the office really quick and then I will be back as soon as possible. While driving to the office I received a call from an unknown number. I decided to answer, and a deep husky male voice asked me if we could meet down at the warehouse on 4th street.

I asked the guy who he was, but he did not answer me, and he told me to be at the warehouse at exactly Eleven before he hung up. I found it odd that this stranger had my number and that he wanted me to meet him at the warehouse, but I knew that it would be rude not to go so I did exactly that. As soon as I finished up at the office around ten, I opened up my left drawer of my desk and I placed my gun under my shirt behind my back.

I did not know what the guy wanted, and I wanted to be prepared in case he tried to do something. I got into my car, and I drove down to the warehouse where I saw that someone was waiting for me. The guy was looking sketchy, so I parked my car, and I cocked my gun before I got out. I walked up to the guy, and he reached out to me with his left hand.

He introduced himself to me and told me that his name is Tony after which I shook his hand, and I told him that my name is Tommy. I asked him why he wanted to meet me, and he told me that everything was going to become clear to me soon enough. I looked at him and frowned. Why on earth would this man be wearing a black jacket in the middle of summer?

Tony looked at me and he told me that he had a job for me. He also said to me that if I was interested then I must meet him here at Ten tonight. I wanted to ask him what the job was, but he disappeared into the warehouse before I could even get a word out. I wanted to follow him, but something told me not to do it, so I walked back to my car, and I drove back to Frank's house.

When I arrived, we had a few drinks and Frank got started on the fire afterwards. Maddie and I left at nine thirty and I drove straight to the warehouse. She asked me what we were doing there, and I told her that she must lock all the doors and that I will be right back. I walked into the warehouse, and I found Tony waiting for me inside.

I walked to him, and I asked him what the job was about, and he handed me a piece of paper with an address on it. He told me that a guy called Eddie owes him a few million dollars and that he wants me to go and pick it up from him. I nodded and walked back to my car. While driving I told Maddie what I had to do right now, and she told me that I should just be careful because I might be walking into a trap.

I stopped outside the house, and I kissed Maddie after which I told her that I am always careful. I walked up to the front door, and I kicked it open. When I walked inside, I called out to Eddie and this tall body builder shaped mother fucker walked towards me. He asked me what I wanted, and I told him that I am looking for a guy called Eddie. He looked down at me and he told me that I am talking to him.

I looked up at him and I told him that Tony sent me to come and collect the money that he owed him. Eddie looked at me and he said that if I wanted the money then I would have to go through him first. After at least half an hour of fighting I bashed Eddie's head in with a cinderblock and I took the bag of cash from underneath the sink.

I walked back to my car, and I drove off. Maddie asked me where all the blood on my face and shirt had come from, and I told her what had happened. I drove back to the warehouse, and I gave the bag to Tony after which he handed me ten thousand dollars. This was my job and I had to do it in order to survive and make a living.

Chapter Four

I could not handle it anymore about how Tony used me to get his money that people owe him and that I had to hurt them, so I went to the police station and I told the cops everything. They told me that if I was willing to help them catch Tony then they will not arrest me, and I immediately agreed.

When I told Maddie what I was planning on doing she tried to stop me and convince me otherwise. She heard about the kind of person that Tony is, and she told me that if I was going to go ahead with this then there was going to be no way that I might make it out alive because Tony is a ruthless guy with no feelings for anyone or anything.

I told her that if I did not co-operate with the cops then they were going to lock me up for working with Tony and I cannot allow that to happen because then I will be away from her for another few years. Maddie's eyes filled up with tears and she told me that she can see that there will not be a way to change my mind so all I had to do was to be careful and to make sure that I return back to her alive.

I wrapped my arms around Maddie for what could maybe be the very last time and I told her that I love her. I then gave her a deep passionate kiss and walked outside to my car. I was extremely scared, but I knew that if I did not do this then I would be behind bars for a very long time. I started my car and made my way to a location near Tony's warehouse where the cops had been waiting for me.

I got into the armored vehicle and Troy placed a small wire on me with a mini microphone strapped to my chest. We hid it so that Tony will not suspect anything, and Troy told me that if I went inside the warehouse in about say five minutes time then I must just act natural. I got out of the vehicle, and I took out a box of cigarettes from my pocket.

I lit myself one as I made my way into the warehouse. Tony was waiting for me on the Northern side of the building with two other guys and I made my way to him. He introduced me to them and told them that if anyone of them had a problem with me then he will take care of it himself. I gulped and we all nodded our heads in agreement.

Tony pulled me to the side where we were being able to talk to each other alone without the other two idiots hearing what we were talking about. Tony told me that he wants to get rid of the two guys and he had a plan. He then kept quiet and smiled at me and I somehow immediately knew what he had planned for them.

Tony looked at me and he told me to go to the harbor and collect some parcels for him. He also said in the same breath that I should hold on to the parcel until we meet at the warehouse again tonight at Eight sharp. I nodded and took in a deep breath. I remembered what Maddie told me about Tony and I started to get second thoughts about this whole thing with the cops.

I greeted Tony and I made my way outside. After making sure that I was not being followed I made my way back to Troy. We spoke for about an hour about how this whole thing was going to go down, and he promised me that he will make sure that his squad will do everything to ensure that I will make it out of this thing alive.

After leaving I made my way to the harbor and I picked up a few crates. When I returned back home, I decided to take a peek at what was in the crates. When I opened it up I froze, inside were at least a dozen weapons and I knew that shit was starting to get real very fast. I closed the crates again and I waited for the time to go meet Tony again.

When the time came, I met up with Troy again and we went over the whole plan. I called Maddie and I told her that I am about to go and take Tony down. She sighed and she begged me to come back alive and to be careful. I told her what Troy said and I could hear by the sound of her voice that she had calmed down a little.

Troy told me that it was time for us to go and I told Maddie that I love her before I hung up. I took in a shaky breath, and I nodded at Troy. I got back into my car and made my way back to the warehouse while Troy and his squad followed a few meters behind to make sure that we do not get seen working together.

When I arrived outside the warehouse I sat in my car for a little while before getting out and taking the crates inside. I knew to myself that this was the end of the line where Troy was finally going to sit with his ass behind bars for a very long time.

Chapter Five

I made my way into the warehouse with the crates and met up with Tony. He told me that they he was going to sell these weapons to a group of people who is much more dangerous than himself. Tony then thanked me for doing a fine job and bringing the weapons to him. We spoke about what time the delivery was going to take place and the location and he told me that he wanted me there with him.

I gulped and looked at him with fear hidden deep in my eyes, deep enough that he could not see it. I wanted to decline going along with him, but before I could get a word out Troy and his squad burst in through the door. Two cops jumped me, and they handcuffed my hands behind my back while Tony tried to run away. Troy followed him and after a short time he came out with Troy in handcuffs as well.

I sighed a slight breath of relieve because I now knew that this thing of me working for Tony was finally over. Tony looked at me and asked me if I had anything to do with this and I shook my head to make him believe that I am innocent. Tony nodded and he told me that I better not have had to do with this because if he had to find out then he was going to make my life a living hell.

Troy took him outside and loaded him into the back of a police car and the officer drove off with him. When I walked outside, I asked Troy if handcuffing me was really necessary and he told me that it was the only way for them to get me out of there alive otherwise Tony would have known that I tipped them off and he would have killed me on that very spot.

I thanked Troy for helping me get away from Tony and for keeping me safe. Troy smiled and he told me that I should not worry about it because they were only doing their job. I shook Troy's hand, and I told him that working undercover with them was fun and all, but I do not think that I will ever be doing it again soon.

I called Maddie and I told her that I am on my way to come and see her. She told me that she will be waiting for me in the backyard because they are busy getting everything ready for a braai. I told her that I will be there soon, and I hung up after which I made my way to my car. I drove down to Maddie's and as soon as I arrived, she ran up to me and jumped up into my arms.

She gave me a deep kiss and she told me that she is glad that I made it out alive. We walked to the backyard and Frank first yelled at me for getting caught up in such big shit with the Tony guy, but then he also congratulated me for making it out alive because not many who double crossed Tony had been as lucky as I was tonight.

I smiled and nodded towards Maddie as I told Frank that I had no choice but to make it out alive because I finally had someone in my life to come back home to. Frank laughed and he told me that if I want to date his daughter then I should not get myself into this type of shit again because the next time I might really end up getting either myself or Maddie killed, and he did not want to see something like that happen.

I looked at Frank and I swore to him that I was not going to get myself into such things ever again. He nodded and handed me an ice-cold beer after which he invited me to stay for the braai and the night. I took the beer and thanked him after which I opened it, and I took a sip. Maddie called me and I made my way to her. When I looked into her eyes I saw fear.

When I asked her what was wrong, she asked me what we were going to do if Tony somehow found out about what I did, and he sends some of his guys on the outside to come get rid of me? I wrapped my arms around her and held her tight to my chest as I told her that none if it will happen because Tony is going away for a very long time and Troy's plan worked like a bomb.

I pulled away slightly and gave Maddie a reassuring kiss that I could feel made her calm down instantly. When I told her that her father gave us the green light to be together and that he invited me to spend the night Maddie ran up to him and she thanked him with a kiss on the cheek and a hug. She made her way back to me and took my hand in hers while entwining our fingers.

I looked at our hands and smiled. I knew that Maddie was the one who I want to spend the rest of my life with. After braaing and eating we made our way upstairs to turn in for the night. I gave Maddie a deep kiss and told her good night.

When I woke up the next morning, I phoned Maddie and told her that I was thinking on applying for becoming a private investigator. She t told me that it was a great idea because it was going to keep me out of trouble with the cops.

I laughed as I told her that it is one of the reasons why I want to do it and that the second reason is because I want to be able to help people. Maddie told me that if there is anyone who she knows that has what it takes to be a private investigator then that person would be me.

According to her I had enough heart and brains to help me out if my application to become a private investigator was successful. I did not argue with Maddie, but I thought to myself that if I was as smart as she makes me out to be then I would not have allowed myself to get caught up in the mess with Tony.

Chapter Six

It has been a few years since I helped the cops to catch Tony and put him behind bars. I had become a private investigator, and everything went well for me and Maddie. We moved in together and we got married soon after. Her family visited us each holiday and her dad cannot stop asking when he was going to get a grandchild from us, and I told him that it is in our plans as a family.

I woke up one morning to the sound of my phone ringing and as soon as I answered a female voice told me that she heard about me from one of my previous clients. She told me that her name is Jennifer and that she is in need of my service. Jennifer told me that if I was willing to help her then she was willing to meet me to discuss the details of the job and she will also give me thirty grand now and the other thirty as soon as the job is done.

I asked her where she wanted to meet, and she told me that we can meet at the coffee shop on Main Street at Ten sharp. I told her that I will be there, and we hung up. When Maddie woke up, she asked me what the call was about, and I told her that I had a new client who needs my help. I told her that she is welcome to tag along if she wanted to.

Maddie told me that she would love to, and she got up to get dressed. As soon as we were dressed, we made our way outside to my car and we drove off. When we arrived at the coffee shop, we made our way inside. I took a look around and saw a woman in a red sparkling dress waving at me. Maddie and I walked to her, and we sat down.

Jennifer thanked me for meeting up with her and she asked me for my bank details. As soon as she finished transferring the thirty grand into my account, we ordered us each a cup of coffee and we started talking business. She told me that her brother had gone missing, and she wanted to know if I can help her to find him.

I asked her who had known him and who he had done business with. Jennifer told me that he had been working for some guy called Mike and the last time she had seen her brother was three days ago. I nodded and asked her if she knew where he always went if he wanted to be alone and she told me that Rico never left her for more than a day and he always called her.

Jennifer took a sip of her coffee, and she then told me that she just hopes that nothing bad had happened. I gave her a reassuring smile as I told her that Rico will be fine and that I will do everything to bring him back to her. We finished our coffee and went our separate ways so that I can start doing what I do best.

Maddie asked me if she could join me this time and she promised that she will not bother me while I am doing my job. I laughed and

I told her that she can join me after which she grinned and thanked me because she had always wanted to know what a private investigator did to find the missing people.

I drove down to Mike's, and we walked inside. I saw a guy working on a car and I walked to him. I asked him if he was Mike and the guy asked me who wanted to know. I told him that my name is Tommy, and I am a private investigator who just wanted to ask him about a guy called Rico. Mike looked at me and he told me that he had not seen Rico since he left after work three days ago.

He told me that he also wants to know where Rico is because he had missed out on a lot of work. I thanked him for his time, and we made our way to my car. As we drove off, I looked at Maddie and I told her that I hope that we will find Rico alive. After a few hours of struggling, I saw a body lying in a field. I stopped and got out of my car, but when I got close to the body I froze. It was Rico and I knew that I had to tell Jennifer what I had found.

I called Jennifer and I told her that I had found Rico, but I had bad news. She immediately knew what I was going to say next, and she burst out in tears. She hung up and transferred the last thirty grand into my account. Two months went by and I got a call from an unknown number. When I answered, I was shocked to hear that it was Tony.

Tony told me that he took one of my hair locks that he found when the cops caught him, and he had it tested. I asked him why he is telling me this and he told me that the results that came back was very interesting. It bothered me how he knew what my number was, and he told me that the results says that I am his son.

I did not want to believe it, so I hung up the phone. Maddie looked at me and she asked me why I had this look of confusion on my face, and I told her what Tony had just said to me. She looked at me with a surprised look on her face and I told her that I do not know if I can trust him and believe what he says. I took my keys and I drove down to prison to go and see him.

We spoke to each other, and I asked him how he can be my father if my dad died when I was a kid. He told me that he had to make me believe that he was dead to protect me, and he showed me the test results. I got mad when looking at it and I stormed out to my car.

Chapter Seven

I jumped into my car and drove off. While driving I tried not to think about Tony and what the DNA results said, but it was hard not to think about it. I decided to stop at a close by shop to pick up a few things for the house that I was going to need to prepare dinner for tonight.

I walked into the store and I bought some meat and a bread. I walked to the fridge and grabbed a twelve pack of beers after which I paid for everything, and I headed back home. As I was driving, I saw a bright ball of lightheaded towards me out of the sky, but I did not think much of it because my mind was preoccupied.

Just before I headed out on the main road the ball of light struck my car and I got crushed underneath it, or so I thought. The meteorite split in half on impact, and I do not know how, but my body somehow absorbed the energy and all of the wounds healed by itself.

When I woke up, I found it strange because I knew that I should have been dead, but I am not. I got up and dusted myself off after which I slowly started walking back home. While walking I noticed a car pulling up next to me. The friendly old man asked me where I was headed and when I told him he offered me a ride.

I got into the car, and we drove off. The old man asked me if I was alright and where my clothes were. I told him what had happened, and he gave me a coat to put on so that I will not get arrested for public nudity. When we arrived outside my house, I thanked the old man for his kindness and help.

I walked inside and found Maddie standing in the kitchen. I walked towards her, and I gave her a hug. She asked me what had happened and when I told her she said that we should go to her uncle who works for the hospital to have me tested. I did not like the sound of that so I told her that we will not be doing no such thing.

Maddie told me that her uncle will be able to help me, and I shook my head. I told her that there is nothing wrong with me and that I am feeling much better than I have ever felt before. Two hours went by, and we decided to order takeaways so that we can eat before going to bed.

While sleeping I felt something strange happening to me. When I woke up the next morning I decided to go and take a shower. I looked at myself in the mirror while taking my shirt off and I froze. I have always been this scrawny guy, but as I took another look in the mirror, I noticed that I now look like a body builder.

I wrapped a towel around me and called Maddie. When she entered into the bathroom, I told her that I have something to show her, and I took off the towel. She checked me up and down and her mouth dropped open because she does not know me to be in this shape.

I took a shower and we headed to the kitchen. Maddie called her uncle, and she told him that we are on our way to come and see him. I was against the idea, but Maddie convinced me to agree so we headed down to the hospital and straight to her uncles office. Jack welcomed us inside and he drew some of my blood for testing purposes.

We spoke to each other, and he asked me a series of questions that I had to provide the answers for. Luckily for us her uncle had a contact in the lab, so my results came back an hour later. When Jack looked at the results he froze after which he looked at me and said that this is incredible.
I sent Maddie out to the cafeteria after which I frowned and asked him what it said. As soon as she left, he told me that I am a superhuman. I burst out laughing and I told him that there is no such thing, but he proofed me wrong. Jack took a knife and he cut me on my arm. He told me to watch and as soon as I looked at the cut it started closing immediately.

I passed out just there and when I finally came to, I was laying on a bed. I sat up straight and Jack came to us to bring me some water so that I can stay hydrated so I took it because I knew that if I did not drink it, I will not hear the end of it from Jack.

I gulped down the water and stood up. Maddie took the car keys, and she told me that she was going to drive us home. I did not want to argue with her, so I just nodded and walked out. While on our way home I noticed a few ambulances and fire trucks blocking a part of the road and when we passed through, I asked Maddie to stop.

I got out of the car and ran towards the chief of the fire station, and I asked him what had happened. Crenshaw told me that there had been a serious accident and that one of the cars that was involved is hanging of the side of the bridge. When I told him that I wanted to help he told me to leave it to the professionals and to head home.

I ran to the car and grabbed it by the bumper after which I pulled it back onto the bridge. Everyone stared at me in amazement as I made my way back to Maddie's car. One guy asked me how I did that, and I told him that I do not know and that I thought that I was doing the right thing.

When Maddie and I got home we saw a video on the news that evening about me pulling the car back onto the bridge. I smiled slightly and looked at Maddie after which I told her that this could work for me. I had this gift and I would rather love to share it with the world and to protect everyone instead of keeping it to myself.

Chapter Eight

It has been a few months since I got this gift and I had slowly but surely started to learn what I can do and how to control it. I called a close friend of mine, and I asked him to create a suit for me with a cape and a mask to hide my identity. Maddie had become a journalist, and I began saving the world without her knowing about it and I kept my identity hidden from everyone.

While Maddie was at work some guy stormed in and he yelled at everyone that he wanted the guy who calls himself Titan. He grabbed Maddie and held her by the arm with her hanging out the window. I made my appearance, and I told him the let her go because I am here now.

As soon as Ryan let her go, she ran straight towards me and hid behind me. Everyone was shocked to see that she knows me, and I looked over at Ryan. He pointed a gun at me, and he told me that this is for not helping when he needed me. I frowned and he told me that he called to me a few weeks ago to safe his brother from a sinking boat, but I did not show up.

I told him that I had to take care of things in Chicago and he laughed. He shot me and I bent over to make him believe that I got hurt, but as soon as the wound closed up, I grabbed him and flew out of the window. When I flew high enough, I told him that he just made the biggest mistake in his life.

He begged me not to kill him and I told him that I am not a murderer. I flew him back down and safely placed him down on the ground where I tied him to a lamp post and told one of the close by people to call the cops as I flew off again.

I stopped by Maddie to make sure if she was alright and she nodded. She asked me if she could take a picture of me because she wants to write an article about me, and I agreed. I picked Maddie up and we flew off together right after she took the picture.

I took her up to the largest building in the world and we sat down on the edge of the roof. Maddie asked me how I got my powers, and I told her that it was a secret because I knew that if I told her then she would know who I really am.

We spoke for a few hours and then I flew her back home. Maddie looked at me and she asked me if she would ever see me again. I smiled at her, and I told her that if she wants to see me again then all she has to do is call out my name.

I flew off to the roof of the house and I quickly changed back into my normal clothes after which I flew back down to the front door and walked inside just as Maddie came it from the porch. She ran up to me and gave me a big hug as she told me about this new superhero called Titan.

I smiled slightly and I told her that I am glad that there is someone who could finally restore peace and order to this world. Maddie told me that he is exactly what this world needs and she also told me how he saved her life.

I decided to make a joke with her, and I asked her if I should be jealous. Maddie laughed and she told me that I should not worry because he is not exactly her type because she loves me, and she will never be able to fall in love with Titan.

Hearing those words come out of her mouth made me want to tell her that I am Titan, but I kept my mouth shut because I knew that if I told her then her life was going to be in danger and that is the exact thing that I am trying to avoid.
Three months went by, and I really started to enjoy this whole saving the world thing. When I woke up one morning, I saw Maddie crying. When I asked her what was wrong, she kissed me and thanked me for the greatest gift that anyone has ever given her.

I frowned as I asked her what she was talking about, and she told me that we are going to be a family. At first, I did not understand what she meant by that, so I just sat there and thought about it. When I realised what she was trying to tell me I froze.

Maddie was pregnant and I was going to be a father. I made a promise to myself and to her that I will do everything in my power to protect her and our child. I was going to be there for my family, and I was also going to make my kid proud to call me his or her dad.

Maddie went off to work as usual and I went about my day saving the citizens. As I was flying around that afternoon, I heard Maddie calling my name. I flew down to her and she told me that she wants to introduce me to her husband.

I did not know how exactly we would pull it off because I am her husband, but she does not know it. I did not want to disappoint her, so I agreed to meet her husband. She asked me to swing by around seven because that is when Tommy will be home.

I nodded and told her that I will see her tonight after which I flew off. When I arrived at her home, she told me that Tommy will be home any second now then she will introduce me to him. I asked her if I could quickly use the bathroom and she told me exactly where to find it, as if I did not already know.

As soon as I entered into the bathroom, I quickly snuck out the window and changed back into my normal clothes. I snuck around to the front door and walked in. Maddie walked to me, and she gave me a kiss after which she told me that she wants to introduce me to Titan, but he was just in the bathroom.

An hour went by, and she told me that she is going to check up on him because he was taking a little bit long in the bathroom. As she walked upstairs towards the bathroom, I snuck out the door and back to the bathroom after which I pulled my suit back on.

I made sure to leave Maddie a message saying that I had to go back to work because there had been an emergency. When she knocked on the door, I opened it and walked out. When we got downstairs, she saw that Tommy was gone and she read the note that I left her.

She looked at me and apologised for wasting my time and that she will have to introduce me to Tommy some other time. I smiled at her, and I told her that it is not a problem. We walked out to the porch, and we bid each other a good night after which I flew off.

I quickly changed back and walked into the front door. I asked Maddie where Titan was so that I could meet him, and she told me that he flew off. I took in a deep breath of relief, and I told her that I will make sure to be here the next time she wants to introduce him to me.

Chapter Nine

Nine months went by, and it became harder to keep my identity hidden from my wife because when Titan was around, I was gone. I got tired of keeping it from Maddie and as I was getting ready to tell her the truth, she asked me to take her to the hospital because our baby was coming.

We made our way out to the car, and I sped off towards the hospital. When we arrived, I called a few nurses, and they took Maddie to the labour room. I went with her, and I stood by her side as she was pushing to get the baby out.

As soon as I heard that small cry coming from the baby it felt like my heart was melting. The doctor handed the baby to me, and he congratulated us on having given life to a beautiful baby girl. I looked at her with tears in my eyes and I gave Maddie a deep passionate kiss.

The doctor asked me what we were going to call our daughter and Maddie looked at him. I told him that we are planning on calling her Lilly. The doctor smiled and told me that he thinks it is a beautiful name for our beautiful little girl.

I looked at Maddie and I smiled. I knew the procedure was to keep her and little Lilly in hospital for the next week to make sure that both of them was alright and healthy. I asked Maddie if she wants anything from the cafeteria and she told me that if I could bring her something to eat and drink then she would appreciate it.

I walked to the cafeteria, and I bought as each a sandwich and two cokes. As I made my way back to Maddie's room, I thought to myself if I should come clean to Maddie and tell her that I am Titan or not. I ran a hand through my hair and walked into the room.

After giving Maddie her sandwich and coke I sat down in the chair right next to her. We ate our food and after that I told her that I have something to tell her. She looked at me and asked me if I also found it weird that I am not around when Titan shows up and how I come back right after he flies off.

I gulped and nodded nervously after which I told her that he might have important things to do. Maddie looked at me and laughed. When I asked her why she was laughing she told me that for a second there she thought that I was Titan.

I laughed and told her that it is the dumbest thing I have ever heard because there was no way that I could be Titan. The week passed quickly and I finally got to take Maddie and

Lilly back home. When we arrived, she told me that she missed being in her own bed.

She took Lilly upstairs and placed her in her cot so that she can sleep. When Maddie came back downstairs, she found me in the kitchen. I poured us each a glass of sweet red wine and we sat down by the dining table.

I knew that if I did not tell Maddie the truth then she was going to be pissed if she had to find out some other way. I looked deep into her eyes, and I told her that I had something that I really needed to tell her. She smiled at me, and she asked me what it was, so I took in a deep breath.

I thought about why I kept the secret from her in the first place and I decided to keep it like that so I told her that I love her with all of my heart and that I was really lucky to have her and Lilly in my life as my new family.

Maddie kissed me and she stood up. I looked at her and told her that I think that we should have a braai to celebrate our little daughter's birth. She agreed and I got everything ready after which I made my way outside to the backyard so that I could get the fire started.

As soon as the fire was ready, I placed the meat on the grill, and I sat down next to Maddie. After a while we dished up and we sat down at the dining table. After eating I washed the dishes, we made our way upstairs. We took a shower together after which we headed straight to bed.

When we woke up the next morning Maddie made her way to Lilly's room to go and feed her. I made my way downstairs and into the kitchen where I made me and Maddie each a cup of steaming hot coffee. Maddie made her way to me, and we drank our coffee.

We kissed each other and I told her that she could stay at home and look after Lilly while I went to work each day. Maddie looked at me and she asked me if I was sure about it. I nodded and I told her that I will see her tonight.

I was lucky because I only worked until four, but Maddie did not know it, so I had enough time to safe people Aswell. While I was flying around after work, I heard a woman screaming and I flew down to her. When I got to her a guy turned around and he held a black bullet made of titanium out towards me.

I did not know how he knew that it was my weakness, but he knew. I fell down to the ground and as he came into the light, I saw that it was the same guy who called me out the newspaper where Maddie works.

I asked him why he was doing this, and he told me that this world does not need a goodie two shoes like me messing everything up for all the criminals. The lady walked towards him, and she told him to stop or else he was going to kill me, but he only looked at her and told her to go home because her work here was done.

As she walked past me, she got tears in her eyes, and she said to me that she was sorry for doing this to me. I managed to get back up to my feet and I kicked the bullet out of his hand. I then punched him hard enough on his jaw to knock him out cold after I flew off back home.

Chapter Ten

As soon as I came close to my house, I crashed into the backyard. Maddie heard the noise, and she came outside to check what was going on. When she saw me, she ran towards me. She asked me if I was alright and I told her that I was fine.

When I tried to stand up to fly away, I fell down again. Maddie told me that I am not fine, and she helped me into the house. She told me that I should spend the night and that she is sure that Tommy will not mind.

I wanted to argue but passed out on the couch. Maddie pulled a blanket over me, and she reached to take my mask off and get me dressed into normal clothes. When she took it off, she froze because she then saw that I am Tommy and also Titan.

When I woke up the next morning, I saw that Maddie was sitting on the couch right opposite me and she was not very happy. When I asked her what was wrong, she yelled at me and asked me why I kept it a secret from her.
I looked at her and pretended not to know what she was talking about. Maddie told me that I can stop playing games because she knows that I am Titan. I sat up and I told her that I did not want her to know because it will endanger her, and Lilly's lives.

She took in a deep breath, and she told me that I could have been honest with her about this whole thing because she felt bad about the fact that she was wasting Titan's time by wanting to introduce him to me and me not being around when he is.

She told me that she thought that she was going crazy because whenever she looked at Titan, she noticed that we had the same facial features, but she never placed two and two together. I walked to her, and I gave her a tight hug as I told her that I am sorry for not telling her the truth.

I begged her not to post my identity in the newspapers because if my enemies found out the I am her husband then they were going to come after her and Lilly and I did not want it to happen. Maddie gave me a deep kiss and she grinned after which she told me that she cannot belief that she is actually married to a superhero.

Seven years passed and we signed Lilly into her first year of school. I asked Maddie not to tell Lilly that I am a superhero because she has my DNA and I do not want her to be treated differently by the other kids if they found out.

We kept it a secret for a long time, but after some time we got tired so I decided to have Lilly meet Titan so that we can reveal my identity to her. We called Lilly downstairs, and we told her that we had someone who we thought she would like to meet.

I walked to the living room and pulled on my suit. I walked back into the kitchen and Maddie told Lilly that I am Titan. Lilly smiled at me, and she told me that she is pleased to finally meet me, and she told me that she heard a lot of stories about me from her mom and her friends.

Maddie smiled at her, and she asked Lilly if she wanted to know what my identity is, and Lilly nodded excitedly. I smiled at her as I pulled of my mask and Lilly froze. She stared at me and grinned after which she shouted that her daddy is a superhero.

Maddie and I laughed, and we told her that she cannot tell anyone who I really am or else she will be treated differently by the other kids. We continued with our lives, and we all lived together in perfect harmony for the rest of our lives.

About the Author

Hi, my name is Jaén-Pierre Bresler, but most people call me JP. I live in Mbombela/Nelspruit, a beautiful city in South Africa that's surrounded by nature reserves and wildlife. As you may have guessed, I love animals.

Only recently did I discover that I have a talent for writing books. It all started as a personal challenge to prove to myself that I could accomplish anything I set my mind to. I never finished school, and for a long time, people told me that I wouldn't be able to do much with my life. But I didn't let their negativity define me.

Writing the book was a challenging but fulfilling experience. It allowed me to tap into my creativity and to express myself in a way that I never thought was possible. It also helped me to grow as a person and to discover new things about myself.

Thanks for reading! I hope that you enjoy it and that it inspires you to chase after your own dreams. If you have any questions or comments, please don't hesitate to contact me at jpbresler21@gmail.com. I'd love to hear from you. If you loved the book and have a moment to spare, I would really appreciate a short review as this helps new readers find my book.